THE GALORE GANG

Mom and Her Magical Robe

GEORGINA FAGAN

Illustrations by Desi D'Amani

**LANDON
HAIL**
PRESS

Thank you, Mom. I couldn't have done it alone.

I'm so grateful I didn't have to.

On a sunny afternoon, Bridget and Ben ran from the school bus toward their house. Mom was waiting by the door.

They both ran quickly past the sprinkler

that was watering the lilies, trying to stay dry.

Mom said, "Hi," and gave them both a hug.

Then she asked Ben and Bridget to get into their pajamas.

"Do I have to, Mom?" Bridget asked. "I didn't even get wet!"

She wanted to watch music videos of her favorite group, CBR, on Mom's phone. She really loved music. She sang into her brush like a microphone while wearing her big pink boa, pretending to be on stage.

Mom always laughed and called her Hollywood!

Ben put on his MagicMaster cape and mask. It was black and yellow with the letters *MM* on the back. He thought it was awesome!

Ben began to pretend to fly around his big sister. MagicMaster was his favorite superhero!

Mom laughed. "Bridget, it's Monday, and I have to go to work at the restaurant tonight. So, you know what that means..."

"We are going to Grandma's house! Yay!"

Mom smiled.

Ben hoped Grandma would take them to the playground near her house, the one next to the train station that went to the city.

"And don't forget to take your tablets, too," Mom said. "You will have to do your homework with Grandma tonight."

"Aww, do we have to?" Ben asked. He began scrolling his tablet, looking for games, instead. He didn't want to do his homework. He just wanted to have fun!

Bridget explained that she had already finished her work. "Mom, can I bring my new nail polish, instead?" She loved to paint Grandma's fingers in different bright, glittery colors! That's Hollywood!

Mom ran back and forth, getting dressed and putting extra clothes and wipes in a bag, in case they got messy. Then she dropped Bridget's hair clip on the floor and picked it up with her toes! Mom was moving so fast!

"Yes, bring your tablet, please," she said. "Grandma can help you with your homework. Now, let's go. I can't be late!"

Mom double-checked their seat belts, locked the doors, and jumped in the car before driving swiftly to Grandma's house.

After they all got
out of the car and ran
up the walkway, Mom
rang the doorbell.
Then she kissed their
foreheads softly.

"Bye, guys. Be good. I love you! I'll see you in a few hours, and then we

can go home to bed!"

Grandma's house smelled like cookies, and it was Ben's job to guess what kind. "Um, chocolate, chip?" he asked.

Grandma looked at him and said, "Boy, you sure know your cookies!"

Bridget already had one in her hand!

"After dinner, Bridget!" Grandma laughed and wiped the yummy chocolate batter from her fingers.

"Dinner is almost ready. Let's start your homework!" Grandma sounded excited. Usually, Mom helped Bridget and Ben do their homework as soon as they got off the school bus. But not

on the nights she had to be at work.

Tonight, Grandma would help out as long as Bridget helped her find Ben's homework on his tablet! Grandma joked she could only work with paper and pencils.

Bridget swiped over to the homework on Ben's tablet for Grandma and then took her nail polish out of her bag. She lined up all the pretty little bottles on the dining room table, getting ready to paint Grandma's toenails like she always did.

But just then, Grandma read Ben's homework assignment, and the smile disappeared from her face.

Ben's assignment was to write about his dad for Father's Day. "What makes your dad a superhero?" was the prompt. Grandma knew this wasn't going to be easy for Ben, since he and Bridget did not get to know their dad growing up, except for in the stories Mom told them.

When Ben read the prompt on his tablet, he looked sad and started to cry.

Grandma gave him a hug and rubbed his head. Bridget felt sad then, too, but she tried to hide it. *Oh boy*, Grandma thought. *Now, what should I do?*

While comforting Ben and rubbing Bridget's head, Grandma thought quickly and suddenly had the best idea!

"Have I ever told you about the superhero who lives in *your* house?"

"What superhero, Grandma?" Bridget asked, looking confused. "We just live with Mommy..."

"I am talking about your mommy!"

Ben and Bridget were confused. They looked at each other and shook their heads. Grandma was being extra silly today!

"No, Grandma, she isn't a superhero. She is just a mom," Ben said, frustrated. "She doesn't even wear a cool costume or a cape or anything!"

Bridget gave him a tissue. "He is right, Grandma. We just have a regular mom!"

Ben wiped his tears and thought about his mom. He knew she worked a lot and sometimes she asked them to play quietly in the mornings, so she could rest.

"Grandma," Ben said, "Mom wears her robe and drinks coffee. That's it!"

"Oh no, sweet boy, that's not it. But you *are* right about one thing. Mom loves her robe because it has *secret* superhero powers!"

"It may look ordinary," Grandma continued, "but her robe is special! All the white moons and yellow stars on her soft, fuzzy robe are magical. They give her energy to be a mommy *and* a daddy for both of you!"

Why when she wears that cozy robe, Mommy can...

Wake up every morning, jump out of bed,

and exercise every day to stay strong and fit.

She can clean the house at lightning speed

all by herself and also

make breakfast and

pack your lunches for

school before you even wake up!

Mommy drives you both to soccer practice, piano lessons, and karate every week, and you are never late. She may not fly, but her car sure does!

She takes you to all your favorite places, like the beach and the park, and she pushes you on the swings higher than everyone else!

Mom magically heals you when you are hurt or sick. She tucks you into bed every night and kisses your head when you are sleeping, but she *never* wakes you up with her Ninja-like skills!

Grandma was right—Mom *is* a superhero!

Both Bridget and Ben smiled broadly. They imagined Mom drinking her big cup of coffee in one gulp and then flying from one task to another!

This made Ben excited now. "She sure is strong," he said.

Bridget was happy, too. "Grandma, does she get all of her powers from her robe?" she asked.

"Not all of them, Bridget. Your love and special hugs give her super-strength, too! That's how she has enough love to be your mommy *and* your daddy!"

Ben grabbed his tablet and ran to Grandma's table. His fingers started to tap on the keyboard excitedly.

Then, he read his sentence out loud, "Happy Father's Day, Mom!" Bridget laughed and helped him... just a little!

Ben felt great now. A big smile shone on his face. He'd never thought about what Mom did before. Everything was magically there for him all the time!

Ben felt really proud and excited about his mom *and* his family.

He remembered what Mom always told him when they felt different from their friends.

"Some families are big," she would say. "Some are small. Our family might look different, but love is around us all!"

Ben couldn't wait to go to school tomorrow and share his story with his class!

When Ben finished his work and dinner was done, Grandma gave them homemade ice cream sandwiches! "Don't tell your mother... It's Grandma's little secret."

After dessert, the door opened, and it was Mom!

"*Mom,*" Ben and Bridget both shouted.

Grandma smiled and wiped crumbs and ice cream from their mouths.

Grandma told Mom how
they'd behaved and that Ben's
homework was already all
done.

The two kids gave Grandma a hug and ran
to Mom's car.

When they got in the car, Bridget whispered to Ben, "Is MightyMaster still your favorite superhero?"

Ben yelled out, "No way! *Mom* is my new favorite superhero, of course!"

Mom chuckled to herself.

Ben asked his mom if she had a favorite superhero, too.

Mom replied, "Well, you know, Ben, a superhero is nothing without their sidekick!"

"That's Grandma!" Bridget and Ben exclaimed.

As they pulled away, the kids turned around to see Grandma waving and

tying the belt to her own fuzzy purple robe!

The End

Special Thanks

There are so many people I want to thank for helping get this book up and running. I would like to start with my mother, Cathy. I love and appreciate you more every day. I never realized how hard it is to be a mom, because you made juggling work and multitasking look like a sport!

I wish my dad was here to be a part of this book with me, but in many ways he was. His stories inspired parts of this book, which makes it extra-special to me. I miss and love you, Dad. Thank you.

Thank you to my now grown children, Cassidy and Matthew. I never knew what pride was until I had you. I love you forever, and I hope that you always know I am here for you. It is my privilege to be your mom, and I can't wait to see you both shine in your adult lives.

Anthony, I wouldn't have been able to sit down and create this at all if not for the life you created for us. I don't say it enough, but I do appreciate you very much, and I loved staying home with Sebastian. It was a luxury I didn't get with Cassidy and Matthew. Your generous heart and nature will always be appreciated by me and our family. I love you.

Sebastian, my son, I love you endlessly. You are the piece of the puzzle that completed our family. I am in awe of you. You are smart, sensitive, and kind and in turn make me want to be a better mother. I will always be here for you, forever and ever.

Thank you to my brother, Pat. I always knew you were smart and talented. I hope you believe it, too! You are a great father to your kids—you remind me of our dad in that way. Your kids are very lucky to have you, and so am I!

To my nephews, Patrick and Ryan, and my niece, Samantha, I appreciate you for all your babysitting and for teaching my kids about baseball and other sports I am clueless about! You are more than family. You are Sebastian's idols. I hope you know we are always here for you when you need it! I love you all.

Special thanks to Jen Widerstrom, my Forena coach and buddy. You are such a big part of my journey in fitness and writing, always giving me a gentle nudge when I need it. I wouldn't have it any other way!

Nicole Sciacca, I told you I always wanted to write a children's book and you said, "*Do it*! So, I did! The pandemic was tough, but the Internet brought new people into my life and I am so glad that you were one of them! Thank you for your light and positivity!

Samantha Joy, your coaching and kindness will never be forgotten. Thank you for holding my hand every step of the way. You always reminded me of how strong I was when I was too scared to see it! This experience was completely out of my comfort zone but you gave me all the tools I needed. I appreciate it all, thank you!

Thank you for all of your beautiful illustrations, Desi d'Amani! I am so impressed with how you turned my memories into art! I will cherish it forever.

Kathryn Galán, you are a complete professional and I thank you for your direction and support. You definitely make it all look easy!

Thank you to all my family and friends. All of you. Through the years, some of you watched my kids so I could work, some have been a shoulder to cry on or someone to laugh with. You are all so special to me, and I love you.

About the Author

Georgina Fagan is a first-time author who makes her writing debut in *The Galore Gang: Mom and Her Magical Robe*. Georgina unexpectedly became a single mother to her two young children, leading her to discover the superpowers within herself, having to be both Mom and Dad. Throughout her years of parenting, she observed her children's inner struggles as they were raised by a single parent and noticed these same challenges in her close friends and family members who were on the single-parent journey. The story of *Mom and Her Magical Robe* is based on events experienced by Georgina and her family. She hopes readers with similar experiences will relate to and connect with the main characters and be reminded that families come in all shapes and sizes. No longer a single parent, Georgina and Anthony, a restauranteur, have blended their family with her now grown children, Matthew and Cassidy, and their son, Sebastian. They live on Long Island, New York.

Desi d'Amani was always doodling and drawing on her notebooks, on scraps of paper, and napkins even, because to her, "it wasn't art, but a language and expression of who I was." In her first art class in high school, her dream of being an "artist" began to stir within. She decided that creating for her life would bring the most to make a happy life. So, she has endeavored to include creativity in every aspect of her life. In 2020, she officially launched DunamisDesi Designs, which extends her passion for creation into a catalyst that fuels and fulfills not only her dreams, but those of her clients. Her work includes children's books, paintings, and murals. With an interactive creative process, she keeps her clients actively involved from concept to creation. When not creating, you can find Desi singing in bands, running, and being an auntie to four lovely kiddos whom she calls her flowers.

Want more Galore?

Please scan this QR code for a fun, free Galore Gang activity!

22044825R00020